Based on the childhood experience of **Georgie Badiel**

THE WATER PRINCESS

Written by
Susan Verde

Illustrated by
Peter H. Reynolds

G. P. Putnam's Sons

I am
Princess
Gie Gie.

My Kingdom . . .

the African sky, so wide and so close.

I can tame
the wild dogs
with my
song.

I can make
the wind play
hide-and-seek.

I can make
the tall
grass
sway
when I
dance.

It is early morning.
Still dark.

My mother wakes me.
"Gie Gie, my princess,
it is time to get up.
We must collect the water."

But the water won't listen, and I know we will have to walk so far to the well.

I am too sleepy
to put on my crown.

I think of the
pot that will rest
on my braids
instead.

The thirst comes quick — dry lips, dry throat.
I squeeze my eyes shut.
I see it.
Clear.
I dip my toes in it.
Cool.
I scoop it up
and bring it to my lips.

Slowly, I open my eyes.
Nothing.

I kick the dust.

I grab my empty pot and place it upon my head. My mother does the same and our journey begins, full of song.

My *maman* adds her melody.
Our steps are light;
we twirl and laugh together.
The miles give us room to dance.

Halfway there,

we stop for a moment at the
giant karite tree, long enough to grab
a handful of sweet shea nuts for energy.

We can keep the dance going
just a little longer.

"Maman, are we there yet?"

Finally, I hear
the water running from the well.
The giggles of my friends.
The chatter of women.

Some have traveled farther than I,

only to return home when
the sun has gone to bed.

Maman holds our place
while I play with friends.
The dance continues.
The water is flowing.

Pots filling
with the dusty-
earth-colored liquid.

The dance home has slowed to careful steps.
My thirst so heavy, like the full pot I carry.
Our song is softer now.

Our shoulders ache; our feet cramp.
I see home at last.

Maman boils enough
water for drinking.
We wait.

We wash our clothes.

We prepare food
for cooking.

My father comes
quickly from the fields
to share in the drink
and the meal.

He scoops me up.

"My princess,
you have returned
with the water."

"Drink,"
Maman says.
Finally.

Every sip fills
me with energy.

I want to make it last,
but I can't.
I gulp it down.

Clothes and body clean,
I sing to the dogs.
I dance with the tall grass.
I hide from the wind.

Maman brings one last cup
she has saved just for me.

"Drink, my princess. Sleep, my princess.

Tomorrow we journey again."

"Maman," I say as I close my eyes.
"Why is the water so far?
Why is the water not clear?

Where is
our water?"

"Sleep," she says.
"Dream," she says.
"Someday you will
find a way, my princess.
Someday."

I am Princess Gie Gie.
My Kingdom?
The African sky. The dusty earth.

And, someday,
the flowing, cool, crystal-clear water.

Someday…

The girls and women of Goundi, Georgie's grandmother's village in Burkina Faso, take the long walk to collect water. They do not yet have a well in their village.

The girls and women of Goundi have arrived at the river, where they fill their pots with water to bring back to the village. The water will still need to be cleaned before they will be able to drink it.

A little girl from Goundi carries water home. She has found the joy and playfulness in the journey; she is a water princess.

Imagine your life without water. No kitchen faucet to fill your glass when you are thirsty. No shower or bathtub to clean your body. Imagine if you couldn't go to school because you had to spend each day walking for miles just to get water and not even know if the water you reach will be clean. This is true for nearly one billion people around the world. That's one out of every six who doesn't have access to clean water.

This crisis is what motivated African model Georgie Badiel to work to make a difference and get clean water to those in need. As a young girl in Burkina Faso, Georgie spent her summers living with her grandmother. Every morning, Georgie and the other girls and women of the village walked for miles to fill pots with water and return it home to be used for the basics—drinking, bathing, cooking—only to wake up the next morning and make the journey again.

Georgie knows firsthand the suffering and struggle of all those without clean water. In Burkina Faso alone, nearly a quarter of the population has no access to clean water. Both illnesses from contaminated water and the time it takes to collect water every day prevent many children from going to school. The walk itself is on average four miles each day, which is the length of about seventy football fields!

The Water Princess is a story inspired by Georgie's own childhood and her wish that the water would come to her and those in her community. Together with Ryan's Well, Georgie is working to make a change and bring this basic right, this source of life, to the people of Burkina Faso and beyond. We hope this story brings awareness to the ongoing crisis and inspires you to be a part of the change.

For more information about what
we can all do to make a difference,
we hope you'll visit us at
www.ryanswell.ca
&
georgiebadielfoundation.org

The children of L'École Primaire de Reo and Georgie Badiel celebrate the first Water Princess well built in partnership with Ryan's Well.

Georgie pumps clean water from the new well at L'École Primaire de Reo, which has about 578 students from six to twelve years old.

The children of Bechialbia play in the water from a new well built by the Georgie Badiel Foundation.

In honor of my grandmother, my mother, my father,
and all the women and young girls around the world
who walk for miles to get water.—G.B.

To all those still waiting and still walking to find clean,
drinkable water and those doing the work to provide access
to this basic human right and precious source of life.—S.V.

To Kathy Loukos.—P.H.R.

G. P. PUTNAM'S SONS
an imprint of Penguin Random House LLC
375 Hudson Street
New York, NY 10014

Text copyright © 2016 by Susan Verde.
Illustrations copyright © 2016 by Peter H. Reynolds.
Photographs © 2016 by Johann Mergenthaler.
Library of Congress Cataloging-in-Publication Data
Verde, Susan. The water princess / written by Susan Verde ; illustrated by Peter H. Reynolds.   pages cm
"Based on the childhood experience of Georgie Badiel."
Summary: "The story of one young girl's quest to bring clean drinking water to her African village"—Provided by publisher.
[1. Water supply—Fiction. 2. Blacks—Africa—Fiction. 3. Africa—Fiction.] I. Reynolds, Peter H., illustrator. II. Title.
PZ7.1.V46Wat 2016   [E]—dc23   2014046250

Manufactured in China by RR Donnelley Asia Printing Solutions Ltd.
ISBN 978-0-399-17258-8
1 3 5 7 9 10 8 6 4 2

Design and hand-lettering by Peter H. Reynolds.
Reynolds Studio supervision by Julia Anne Young.
The art was done in watercolor, gouache and digital inks.